For Lulu, Eileen, Adi and Russell —T. M.
To my aita —E. O.

Published by
PEACHTREE PUBLISHERS
1700 Chattahoochee Avenue
Atlanta, Georgia 30318-2112
www.peachtree-online.com

ISBN 1-56145-371-4
Text copyright © 2006 by Tom MacRae
Illustrations copyright © 2006 by Elena Odriozola

First published in Great Britain in 2006 by Andersen Press.

Printed and bound in Singapore by Tien Wah Press.
10 9 8 7 6 5 4 3 2 1
First Edition

Library of Congress Cataloging-in-Publication Data

MacRae, Tom.
  The Opposite / written by Tom MacRae ; illustrated by Elena
Odriozola.
     p. cm.
  Summary: Nate wakes up one morning to find The Opposite standing
on his bedroom ceiling, and it causes him trouble at home and at
school, changing what Nate wants to do into its opposite, until Nate
finds a way to outwit it.
  ISBN 1-56145-371-4
  [1. Behavior--Fiction. 2. Assertiveness (Psychology)--Fiction. 3.
Humorous stories.] I. Odriozola, Elena, ill. II. Title.
  PZ7.M24728Opp 2006
  [E]--dc22
                              2005027945

The
Opposite

By Tom MacRae

Illustrated by Elena Odriozola

PEACHTREE
ATLANTA

When Nate woke up one morning,
The Opposite was standing on
the ceiling, staring down at him.

"You can't stand on the ceiling,"
said Nate. "Get down!"

But then The Opposite
happened, and it stayed
where it was.

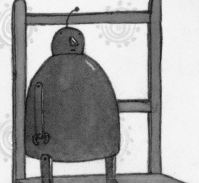

"Dad!" cried Nate. "There's an Opposite on the ceiling!"

"Where?" said Nate's father, poking his head around the door.

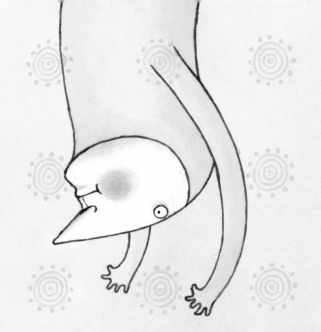

"*There!*" said Nate, pointing up.

But then The Opposite happened, and it wasn't there anymore.

"Come on, Nate," said his father.
"You don't usually make up stories
to stay in bed."

Nate came downstairs for breakfast. His mother filled his bowl with cornflakes. "You can add the milk yourself," she said. Nate always poured his own milk. He was very good at it.

Nate picked up the carton in both hands and gently poured the milk over the cereal.

But then
The Opposite
happened and…

...instead of the milk pouring down, it poured *up*, splashing against the ceiling and then dripping down all over the tablecloth. The Opposite grinned in the corner.

"Oh, Nate!" said his mother. "Look what you've done!"

"It wasn't me!" cried Nate, pointing to the corner. "It was The Opposite!" But The Opposite had already happened, and it wasn't there anymore.

"Come on, Nate!" said his mother. "You're not usually so clumsy."

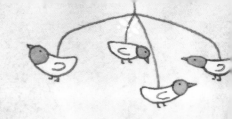

At school, Nate's teacher asked the children to paint a picture of their favorite animal. Nate got out his paint and paper and brush, and started to make an elephant.

But then The Opposite happened and instead of the paint going on the paper, it went on Nate's head.

Then on the floor.

Then on the walls.

Then on his teacher.

The paint went everywhere, except on the paper, which stayed blank and clean.

The Opposite crouched under the teacher's desk and giggled.

"Oh, Nate!" said his teacher. "You're not usually so messy."

"It wasn't me!" cried Nate, pointing under the desk. "It was The Opposite. He's under there!"

But then The Opposite
happened, and it wasn't
there anymore.

Nate thought for a moment. He
had an idea. Slowly, he pointed at
the empty space in front of him.

"I mean," said Nate,
"that there *isn't* an Opposite
standing right in front
of me."

*And then
The Opposite
happened.*

Suddenly,
The Opposite
was standing
right in front
of Nate.

It blinked with
surprise,

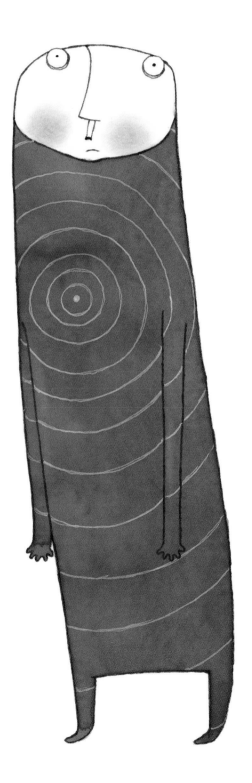

and
looked
a little
worried.

"The work I have done today is messy and untidy," Nate announced.

And then The Opposite happened.

The Opposite bared its teeth, but it was too late. Nate's painting was now as tidy and perfect as you please.

"And," said Nate, smiling, "I have *so* enjoyed having The Opposite with me today and I *do* hope it will stay around forever and ever and *ever!*"

And then The Opposite happened.

With a *shriek*...

...and a *hiss*,

The Opposite disappeared in a puff of green and yellow smoke.

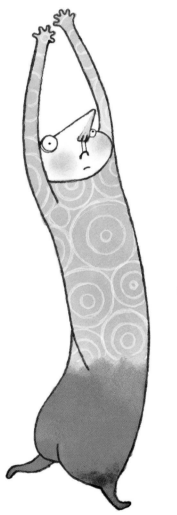

And that was that. Very quickly,
Nate's teacher and class persuaded
themselves that they had never seen
The Opposite and that none of it had
ever happened.

But Nate knew what had happened,
and now you do too. And if you
ever meet an Opposite, you will
know how to deal with it.

When Nate woke up the next morning,
The Opposite was standing on his
ceiling, staring down at him.

"Oh good"
said Nate.
"I hope this
story goes on
forever and
ever...

THE END!"